MISSING!

Flame

Have you seen this kitten?

Flame is a magic kitten of royal blood, missing from his own world.
His uncle, Ebony, is very keen that he is found quickly.
Flame may be hard to spot as he often appears in a
variety of fluffy kitten colours but you can recognize him
by his big emerald eyes and whiskers that crackle with magic!

He is believed to be looking for a young friend to take care of him.

Could it be you?

If you find this very special kitten please let Ebony,
ruler of the Lion Throne, know.

Sue Bentley's books for children often include animals or fairies. She lives in Northampton and enjoys reading, going to the cinema, and sitting watching the frogs and newts in her garden pond. If she hadn't been a writer she would probably have been a skydiver or brain surgeon. The main reason she writes is that she can drink pots and pots of tea while she's typing. She has met and owned many cats and each one has brought a special sort of magic to her life.

Magic Kitten

A Splash
of Forever

SUE BENTLEY

Illustrated by Angela Swan

PUFFIN

To Pixie and Fonzie – crazy tabby clowns

PUFFIN BOOKS

Published by the Penguin Group
Penguin Books Ltd, 80 Strand, London WC2R ORL, England
Penguin Group (USA) Inc., 375 Hudson Street, New York, New York 10014, USA
Penguin Group (Canada), 90 Eglinton Avenue East, Suite 700, Toronto, Ontario, Canada M4P 2Y3
(a division of Pearson Penguin Canada Inc.)
Penguin Ireland, 25 St Stephen's Green, Dublin 2, Ireland (a division of Penguin Books Ltd)
Penguin Group (Australia), 250 Camberwell Road, Camberwell, Victoria 3124, Australia
(a division of Pearson Australia Group Pty Ltd)
Penguin Books India Pvt Ltd, 11 Community Centre, Panchsheel Park,
New Delhi – 110 017, India
Penguin Group (NZ), 67 Apollo Drive, Rosedale, North Shore 0632, New Zealand
(a division of Pearson New Zealand Ltd)
Penguin Books (South Africa) (Pty) Ltd, 24 Sturdee Avenue, Rosebank,
Johannesburg 2196, South Africa

Penguin Books Ltd, Registered Offices: 80 Strand, London WC2R ORL, England

puffin.com

First published 2008
1

Text copyright © Sue Bentley, 2008
Illustrations copyright © Angela Swan, 2008
All rights reserved

The moral right of the author and illustrator has been asserted

Set in Bembo
Typeset by Palimpsest Book Production Limited, Grangemouth, Stirlingshire
Made and printed in England by Clays Ltd, St Ives plc

British Library Cataloguing in Publication Data
A CIP catalogue record for this book is available from the British Library

ISBN: 978-0-141-32349-7

Prologue

As a terrifying roar rang out, there was a bright flash and a dazzling shower of sparks. Where the young white lion had stood there was now a tiny, fluffy grey and white kitten with bright emerald eyes.

Flame trembled, hoping that his kitten disguise would protect him from his uncle. Keeping his belly low to the ground, he crept into the entrance of a nearby cave and hid behind a large rock.

Outside Flame could hear heavy paws thudding over the stony ground. A dark shadow with a thick mane appeared at the mouth of the cave.

'Ebony!' Flame gasped, pressing his tiny body more tightly against the sheltering rock.

The adult lion sniffed the air and gave a low growl as it came into the cave. Flame stiffened. This was it! He was going to be found and dragged outside.

Suddenly a huge paw, as big as Flame was now, reached round the rock and scooped the kitten out.

'Prince Flame. I am glad to see you

again, but it is not safe for you to be here,' the adult lion rumbled.

'Cirrus!' Flame mewed with relief. 'I thought my uncle had found me!'

Cirrus's grey muzzle crinkled in a fond smile as he encircled the kitten with his powerful paws. 'While I live I will protect you, but Ebony will never stop looking for you. He wants to keep ruling in your place.'

Flame's emerald eyes flashed with anger. 'Perhaps it is time for me to face him and take back the Lion Throne!'

'Bravely said,' Cirrus growled softly, his tired eyes narrowing with pride. 'Use this disguise and go back to hide in the other world. Return when you are strong and wise and *then* save the land from your uncle's evil rule.'

Before Flame could reply, a
thunderous roar split the air. There
came the sound of mighty paws on
rock and the ground shook as a heavy
animal jumped to the ground outside
the cave.

'Ebony is very close. Go, Flame. Save
yourself!' Cirrus urged.

Bright silver sparks ignited in the tiny,
fluffy grey and white kitten's fur. Flame
whined softly as he felt the power
building inside him. He felt himself
falling. Falling . . .

Chapter
★ONE★

As Alice Forester listened to her class
teacher, she felt her heart sinking.

'Now that the new pool's ready
for use, we'll be starting swimming
lessons tomorrow. So don't forget your
swimming kit!' Miss Ritson said.
She had a bright, smiley face and very
straight brown hair that she wore
tied back.

'Oh, that's just what I need – not!'
Alice grumbled. She had only just
moved to this school and had been
really pleased to find that she wasn't
going to be having swimming lessons.

Her tummy had gone all squirmy at
the thought of the pool of blue
chlorine-scented water. *It's all right for
the other kids*, she thought. *No one's going*

to bully them *for being better than everyone else at swimming.*

'Yay! I can't wait to get in the new pool. We can do mega dive-bombs and shoulder-stand fights in the shallow end!' shouted Tim Wagnall.

'Now, Tim. You know very well that that kind of dangerous behaviour isn't allowed,' Miss Ritson said, giving him one of her looks.

'Shame!' Tim said cheerfully.

Everyone laughed and even Alice found herself grinning. Tim was always messing about and playing tricks. He could be annoying sometimes, but he was really quite funny.

'And I've got even more exciting news,' Miss Ritson went on. 'We're having a grand reopening ceremony for the new pool and as part of that there's going to be a swimming gala. Everyone's going to take part!' She smiled brightly at the class. 'I can see a few of you looking a bit concerned, but don't worry. There's a new after-school swimming club on Mondays, Wednesdays and Fridays. I'll be coaching and I'd like you all to try to come to a couple of sessions.'

Some of the kids cheered. Tim stood up and ran about windmilling his arms as if he was doing the front crawl, which made everyone laugh again.

Everyone except for Alice. She felt as if her grin had frozen on her face. This was her worst nightmare coming true.

Miss Ritson clapped her hands for silence. 'Calm down, everyone. I'd like you to take out your books and start work please.' As the class settled down, she came over to Alice's desk. 'Are you feeling OK, Alice? I noticed that you looked a little anxious when I was making the announcements.'

'I'm not, Miss,' Alice said. 'It's because . . . I'm . . . er, not allowed to go swimming. I've got this . . . um, really thin blood. It's awful, Miss. The minute I get in the water my legs go all white and wobbly, like cooked spaghetti, and my lips go blue and swell up like great big slimy slugs.'

Miss Ritson frowned. 'That sounds alarming. I assume we have a doctor's letter about that or a note from your mum, excusing you from swimming? I'll check the school records.'

Alice gulped. 'I haven't exactly been to the doctor. And Mum did write a note, but I lost it when . . . um, a dog grabbed it and ran away with it on the way to school.'

'Is that right?' Miss Ritson said, looking sceptical.

'Yes,' Alice carried on desperately. 'And I probably can't come to after-school club either. I have to meet my brother from school and get his tea. Mum's a single parent and she childminds Esme and Luke in the week so . . .'

Miss Ritson smiled patiently. 'I'm fully aware of your home situation, Alice. Swimming club will be open until 8 p.m. I'm sure if you explain to your mum how important this is, she'll make sure you can fit in an hour's practice here and there.'

'Yes, Miss,' Alice mumbled glumly as the teacher moved away.

She sighed, wishing that her best friend from her old school, Holly, was still here. She would understand.

Alice felt her eyes prick with tears, but swallowed hard and began outlining a swirling Celtic design in black felt tip.

Tim Wagnall sauntered past her desk. Reaching back with one hand, he flipped Alice's workbook on to the floor.

'Oh!' Alice's black felt tip had skidded across the diagram, ruining all her careful work. 'You idiot! I'll have to do it all again now!' she said crossly.

'Tough!' Tim sniggered.

As Alice bent down to pick the book up Tim booted it so it slid further under her desk. Alice had to get down on her hands and knees to reach for it.

Tim was still standing there with a silly grin on his face when she sat down again. 'Clear off then,' she said irritably.

Tim rolled his eyes, before walking away. 'Huh! Some people can't take a joke.'

'Yeah? Well you're about as funny as catching the plague!' Alice muttered under her breath.

A minute later, a rubber band pinged on to Alice's arm. When she looked over at Tim he was innocently looking out of the window.

When the bell went for the end of school, Alice headed for the path that led round to her brother Ben's classroom. The school garden filled the square space between the two school buildings. Still worrying about the swimming gala, Alice wandered through the peaceful garden past some rows of tall green beans.

Just as she reached a wooden garden seat, there was a bright flash and a big spurt of silver sparks.

'Oh!' Alice blinked, blinded for a moment.

She looked over her shoulder to see if Tim Wagnall was lurking about. It would be just like him to follow her and set a firecracker off as a prank, but there was no one else around.

When Alice turned back to the garden seat, she saw a tiny kitten with grey and white fur, a cute pink nose and emerald eyes. Hundreds of tiny sparkles, like miniature fireflies, gleamed in its fluffy coat.

Alice frowned. She was sure that she hadn't seen a kitten there a minute ago.

'Where've you just come from?' she murmured wonderingly.

The kitten stood up and arched its tiny back. 'I have come from far away. Can you help me?' it mewed.

Chapter
★ TWO ★

Alice stared down at the kitten in surprise. She must be hearing things. She was sure there was no one else in the garden who could be playing a prank on her.

Alice reached for the kitten to pick it up. *It's just a normal kitten – probably a stray*, she told herself. Its grey and white fur was warm, and soft as thistledown, and she felt a tiny, fast heartbeat ticking against her fingers.

'Please, can you help me?'

Alice's eyes widened with shock at the little voice. She put him down hastily but gently and took a step back. 'H-how c-come you can talk?' she stammered.

The kitten pricked its tiny ears. 'In my world all the big cats can talk. My name is Prince Flame. What is yours?' it mewed again.

Alice gulped. Talking cats did not just appear to ordinary schoolgirls in school gardens! But this kitten had and it was blinking up at her expectantly, waiting for her answer.

'I'm A-Alice Forester,' she found herself replying.

'Alice, I am honoured to meet you,'
the kitten purred. 'Where is this place?'
Despite his tiny size, Alice thought that
Flame seemed strangely unafraid of her.

'Meldway School. In Northampton,'
she replied. 'That's my classroom behind
us.' She felt confused. 'Did . . . did you
just say that you're *Prince* Flame?'

The kitten lifted its head and its
bright emerald eyes gleamed with pride.
'Yes. I am heir to the Lion Throne. But

my Uncle Ebony has stolen it from me and rules in my place.'

Alice was still having trouble taking this all in. 'No offence, but you seem a bit small to be the ruler of anywhere,' she said.

Flame drew himself up indignantly. 'Stand back, please.'

As Alice stepped backwards, Flame jumped down from the bench. There was another bright flash and a big whoosh of silver sparks that crackled as they hit the grass.

'Oh!' Alice was blinded for a moment.

When her sight cleared, she saw that in the tiny kitten's place stood a regal young white lion. Its thick velvety coat looked as if it had been sewn with thousands of twinkling stars. Then just

as suddenly as the majestic lion had
appeared, Flame returned as the fluffy
grey and white kitten with a cute pink
nose.

'Flame? Was that you?' Alice gasped.
'You really are a lion prince!'

Flame nodded and she could see that
his tiny kitten body was starting to
tremble. 'I am in danger from my
uncle's spies. If they find me, they
will kill me. Will you keep me safe?'

Alice felt her heart go out to him. As
a young white lion Flame was awesome.
Disguised as this cute fluffy kitten he
was adorable. 'Oh, of course I will. You
can come and live with me.'

More confidently this time, she
picked him up and gently stroked the
top of his head. Flame began purring

and rubbing his head against her arm.

'Hey! I thought you were supposed to be meeting me!' called an annoyed voice.

Alice looked round to see a six-year-old blonde boy running towards her. It was Ben. Her brother got his blue eyes and floppy fair hair from their mum. Their dad had had brown eyes and springy dark hair. Alice took after him.

'What are you doing over here?' Ben asked and then he saw Flame. 'Cool! Where did you get that kitten?'

'I was on my way over to meet you when I found him. He's called Flame. And he can ta—' Alice began, but suddenly Flame reached up and tapped her cheek with one tiny front paw.

'Miaow-ow-ow!' he said loudly,

looking up at her with pleading emerald eyes and shaking his head.

Alice looked down at Flame, confused, before suddenly realizing that he didn't want her to tell Ben about him. She patted him reassuringly, letting him know that she understood.

Ben looked at Flame with puzzled blue eyes. 'Why's it making that noise? Can I stroke it? Are we going to take it home?'

'Him, not it. And he's got a name,' Alice corrected. 'Yes, we're taking Flame home. He can live in my bedroom,' she said, but then she remembered their mum's strict rules about not having pets. 'Listen to me, Ben,' she said, kneeling down to look him in the eyes. 'This is really important. We're not going to tell Mum about Flame, OK?'

'Great. Flame's dead cute, isn't he? We can share him,' Ben said, not really paying attention.

'Ben! If Mum finds out about Flame, she'll make us take him to the pet care centre. Do you understand that?' Alice said seriously.

'Course I do!' Ben said. 'I won't tell *anyone* about him. Cross my heart and hope to die!'

'OK then. And you have to do what I tell you with Flame. No grabbing him and taking him out to play in the garden or dashing round to your friend's house with him, without asking me first.'

'I don't see why you're in charge!' Ben said, sticking out his bottom lip.

'It's because I found Flame and anyway I'm older than you. Deal?' Alice said.

Ben kicked at some grass with the toe of his trainer. He nodded. 'Deal.'

Alice gave a relieved sigh. 'Right. Let's go home.' She opened her shoulder bag, so Flame could jump inside. 'There you are. Nice and safe,' she whispered as he settled down.

As she and Ben started for home,

Alice put her hand inside her bag and stroked Flame. He was curled up beside her pink velvet pencil case. She smiled as she felt him purring contentedly, but she wished that Ben didn't know about him.

There was nothing she could do about it now. She hoped like mad that Ben would remember his promise not to tell anyone about Flame – especially their mum.

'Hi, Mum, we're home!' Alice called as she and Ben came into the house.

'Hi, Mum. Laters!' shouted Ben, clumping straight upstairs.

'Hello, you two!' Mrs Forester's voice floated out of the kitchen.

Alice popped her head round the

door. Her mum was cooking supper. Esme and Luke sat in their high chairs, picking at little piles of carrot, apple and grated cheese.

'How are the terrible twins?' Alice said, bending down to give them each a kiss on the cheek. 'Have you been good for my mum today? Have you then?'

The twins gave her gummy grins. Esme held up a tiny bit of carrot between her finger and thumb. 'Ally want?'

'Mmm. Yum, yum. Delicious,' Alice said, nibbling at the chubby fingers and pretending to eat.

As Esme squealed with delight, Mrs Forester smiled and tucked a strand of her curly fair hair behind her ears. 'It feels like it's been a long day,' she said with a sigh. 'How was school?'

'OK. Nothing special,' Alice said vaguely, deciding not to mention anything about the dreaded swimming lessons, the after-school swimming club or the gala. Somehow all that seemed a lot less important than finding Flame.

'I'm just going upstairs to get changed, Mum. I won't be a minute,' she said as she went into the hall. She looked inside her bag as she went upstairs. 'I'll make you a cosy bed on my duvet, Flame.'

'Thank you, Alice,' Flame mewed softly. 'I am feeling tired after my long journey.'

Ben followed Alice into her bedroom. 'Get Flame out. I want to play with him,' he cried eagerly.

'Shhh! Mum'll hear you,' Alice
whispered. 'Not now. Let Flame settle
in first. He said that he's . . . I mean
he's probably tired,' she corrected herself
hastily. 'Kittens need lots of sleep you
know.'

'But I want to play with him now,'
Ben protested.

29

'Well you can't. Maybe later,' Alice said firmly.

'He's my kitten too. Not just yours!' Ben snapped.

Alice made herself answer calmly. 'Course he is. Why don't you come with me to buy Flame some food later?'

Ben brightened. 'OK then. Can I choose what sort he has?'

Alice nodded.

Ben went towards the door. 'I'm going to ask Mum if I can go to Dean's house to play now.'

'Don't say a word to him about Flame,' Alice cautioned. 'Dean's mum talks to our mum.'

'I'm not stupid!' Ben scoffed, leaving her room.

Alice heard him go into the

bathroom and close the door. A minute later, the loo flushed and she heard taps being turned on. Ben came out and went downstairs.

Alice sat on her bed beside Flame who was pedalling the duvet with his tiny grey and white front paws. 'Ben's already being a pain about you living here. But at least he thinks you're just a normal kitten.'

Flame nodded. 'It is good that you did not tell Ben about me. You must never tell anyone my secret. Promise me, Alice.'

Alice nodded. 'No one's ever going to hear about you from me, I promise. You're safe with me.'

'Thank you, Alice. I think I will have a nap now.' Flame gave her a whiskery grin and tucked his nose into his paws before settling down to sleep.

As Alice looked at him a bubble of happiness rose up from inside her. In her wildest dreams, she had never imagined that her new best friend would be a magic kitten!

Chapter
★THREE★

Leaving Flame on her bed, Alice
quickly changed into jeans and a T-shirt
and went downstairs.

In the kitchen, her mum was giving
Esme and Luke some drinks in plastic
cups.

Alice filled the kettle at the sink. 'I'll
make us some tea.'

Her mum smiled. 'Lovely! I could

really do with one. The twins' mum has just phoned to say she's stuck in traffic on the motorway, so she could be an hour late. I said Esme and Luke could have supper with us.'

Alice thought her mum looked tired. Ben was a handful, even without looking after two toddlers all day.

Alice checked the saucepan on the stove. 'I think these potatoes are done. Shall I mash them?'

'Would you, love? Thanks,' Mrs Forester said.

'That's OK,' Alice said.

She liked helping her mum. It made her feel grown-up. After she'd made the tea and mashed the potatoes, Alice started on the washing up.

'I think Luke needs changing. I'll take him to the bathroom.' Mrs Forester lifted the little boy out of his chair.

Just then, Alice saw a big drop of water plop on to the draining board. She frowned as another drop splashed next to it, and then another. Looking up at the ceiling, she saw another drop squeezing through a tiny hole. 'Mum, look! Water's dripping from somewhere!'

Mrs Forester glanced up and gave a cry of dismay. 'It's coming from the bathroom. Someone's left a tap running!'

'And I know who. Ben!' Alice was already half out of the kitchen and hurtling up the stairs.

As she reached the landing, she saw water pouring out from the open bathroom door.

'May I help?' Flame mewed from her bedroom doorway, looking bright-eyed and alert after his nap.

'Mum's right behind me! It's probably best if you just hide,' she whispered.

Flame gave a determined purr and time seemed to stand still.

Alice watched in amazement as huge

bright silver sparks ignited in Flame's grey and white fur and his whiskers crackled with electricity. She felt a warm prickling sensation down her spine.

Something strange was going to happen!

In what seemed like slow motion, Flame leapt towards the bathroom, trailing sparks like a silver comet. 'Do not worry. I will use my magic to make myself invisible. Only you will be able to see and hear me, Alice!'

Alice went into the bathroom and stood there in wonderment.

Flame stood on the edge of the bath, balancing on his back legs. Silver sparks were shooting out of his front paws and filling the entire bathroom. They whirled around busily, like millions of little bright worker bees.

Squeak! The hot and cold taps turned themselves off. Shloop! The water in the basin was slurped backwards down the plughole. Sploosh! A big silver cape of water droplets rose from the carpet and swirled itself into the bath, where it collapsed and drained away.

'Wow! This is *so* amazing!' Alice breathed.

Flame jumped down from the bath and stood beside Alice. Just as the last bright spark faded from his fur, Mrs Forester appeared at the top of the stairs, carrying Luke.

She gaped at the spotless bathroom.

'So, where's that water in the kitchen coming from?'

'Condensation,' Alice blurted out. 'We did an experiment on it last term.'

She bit back a grin at the thought that Flame was sitting there large as life, but her mum obviously couldn't see him!

'I suppose it's possible,' Mrs Forester said, looking puzzled. 'Oh well, I'm just glad we haven't got a full-scale flood on our hands. I'd better see to Luke. Could you go down and keep an eye on Esme for me please, love?'

'Sure thing!' As Alice went downstairs, Flame scampered after her. As soon as they were alone, she picked him up and cuddled him. 'Thanks, Flame. You were brilliant!'

Flame rubbed his head against her hand. 'You are welcome.'

The following morning Alice woke to the sound of loud purring close to her ear. Rubbing her eyes, she sat up and reached out to stroke Flame. 'Did you sleep well?'

Flame stuck all four paws out and stretched his legs. 'Yes, thank you. I feel safe here,' he mewed.

'Good. Maybe your uncle's enemies will stop looking for you,' Alice said, gently stroking his tiny ears. 'Then you can stay here forever.'

A troubled expression crossed Flame's tiny face. 'Ebony's spies will not stop until they find me. But even if they passed me by, I could not stay. I must return to my own world one day and take back my throne. Do you understand that, Alice?'

Alice nodded. She felt a pang of sadness at the thought of losing her friend, but she didn't want to think about that now.

Before she could say anything, the bedroom door flew open and Ben ran in. He leapt on to the bed and started making a noisy fuss of Flame. 'I want

Flame to sleep on my bed tonight,' he exclaimed.

'Maybe we should see what Flame wants to do,' Alice said.

'He wants to sleep with me, don't you, Flame?' Ben said. Grabbing the tiny kitten, he rolled him on to his back and began roughly tickling his white tummy.

Flame squirmed and yowled in protest.

'Careful! You're hurting him, you clumsy thing!' Alice snapped, pulling at her brother's arm. 'Flame's only tiny. You have to be very gentle with him.'

Ben's face darkened and he thrust Flame at Alice. 'You never let me do anything with him!' he said, stamping out of her room.

'Are you OK?' Alice asked Flame worriedly.

Flame nodded, shaking out his ruffled fur. 'I am fine. Ben just surprised me. I do not think that he meant to hurt me.'

Alice bit her lip. Flame was right. Perhaps she was being over-protective. Ben was excited about Flame too in his own way.

'Make sure you hide well while I'm at school, won't you?' she said to Flame, a few minutes later.

He looked up at her with bright intelligent eyes. 'I will come to school with you, Alice.'

'Really? But –' Alice stopped mid-sentence as she remembered that only she could see Flame when he used his magic to make himself invisible. She grinned. It would be fun having her secret friend with her all day. 'All right then. Why not?'

Chapter
★ FOUR ★

As Alice was finishing putting on her
uniform, she remembered about the
swimming lesson. Her tummy lurched
and she felt nervous just thinking
about it.

'Is something wrong?' Flame mewed.

Alice explained about being teased by
some girls at her old school who had
been jealous about her being so good at

swimming. 'I used to like going swimming before that. Now I'd just rather not bother. Maybe I could leave my swimming kit here and pretend I forgot it.'

Flame blinked at her. 'Will that mean that you do not have to go into the pool?'

'Probably not. Miss Ritson will just make me wear one of the school's spare costumes, and they're really awful. Anyway, she's on a mission to get us all ready for the gala now. I can't see how I can get out of it.'

She sighed deeply as she stuffed her swimming things into her school bag.

'Perhaps your mum will be able to help,' Flame suggested.

'I don't want her to know that I still

feel like this. She'll only get all worried,'
Alice said.

She hurried downstairs with Flame at
her heels. 'You'd better stay invisible for
now, in case Mum sees you,' she
whispered to him.

Flame nodded.

Ben was sitting at the table eating a bowl of his favourite cereal. As Alice sat down, her mum put a plate of toast on the table. Alice didn't feel like eating much, so she nibbled a tiny corner of toast.

'Are you feeling all right, love? You look a bit pale,' her mum commented.

'I'm OK,' Alice fibbed.

Mrs Forester frowned. 'You're sure nothing's worrying you?'

'Um . . .' The doorbell went before Alice could reply.

Ben dashed to the door. 'I'll get it!'

'That'll be Esme and Luke,' Mrs Forester said, distracted now that the twins had arrived. She went to speak to their mum.

'Phew! That was lucky,' Alice said to

Flame. 'I thought Mum was going to ask me loads of questions.'

Ben bounded back to the kitchen table. 'Where's Flame?' he said loudly. 'I want to give him some milk before school.'

'Give who some milk?' Mrs Forester asked, as she brought Esme and Luke through to the kitchen.

'That kitt– Ow! What did you do that for?' Ben complained as Alice gave him a kick from under the table.

'Come on, Ben. We'll be late for school,' she said, giving him a fierce look.

'But you've got ages before school starts,' her mum said, looking puzzled.

'I know. I just want to get there early today . . .' Alice mumbled vaguely as she

49

grabbed Ben's arm and hustled him into the hall. 'You daft twit!' she scolded, when they were alone. 'You nearly gave the game away!'

Ben's face fell. 'I didn't mean to.'

'I know you didn't,' Alice said, more calmly. 'And I didn't mean to have a go at you. Luckily, Mum didn't really hear you. But we'd better go before she starts asking awkward questions.'

'OK,' Ben said, shouldering his school bag. 'Where *is* Flame, anyway? I've been looking everywhere for him.'

'Oh, he's probably under my bed asleep,' Alice fibbed. There was no way she could tell Ben that Flame was sitting on the doormat, right behind him – invisible to everyone except her!

'There are loads of kids about and it can be slippery round the pool,' Alice said to Flame worriedly, as she was getting changed. 'You could get trodden on or something.'

The girls' changing rooms had new white tiles and smelt of fresh paint. The sound of her classmates' voices echoed outside Alice's cubicle.

Flame was sitting on Alice's folded

uniform. 'I will be very careful to stay out of the way. It will be interesting to watch humans swim.'

Alice nodded.

Flame's furry brow wrinkled in a frown as Alice pulled on her swimming costume and then tucked her hair inside her nylon swimming hat. 'Why do humans need to put on a second skin to get into the water?'

'A second . . . Oh, you mean my swimming costume. I can hardly go swimming with nothing on! I'm not wearing a fur coat like you!' Alice said, grinning. 'And we have to wear swimming caps. It's the rules. But to tell the truth they're a bit useless for keeping your hair dry.'

As Alice headed for the foot bath at

the entrance to the pool, Flame went
off in the opposite direction.

Miss Ritson was at the poolside,
bending down to give instructions to
the swimmers already in the water. She
wore a white T-shirt and track pants
and had a whistle round her neck. Her
straight brown hair was tied in two
bunches.

Some other teachers were with their
classes in different parts of the pool.

Alice walked quickly over to the steps
leading down into the shallow end,
hoping to get into the water before
Miss Ritson spotted her and made a
fuss. But there was a queue of kids
waiting at the steps and Alice had to
wait her turn.

Miss Ritson straightened up. She

looked round and saw Alice. 'Ah, Alice,' she said, coming over. 'I haven't forgotten our conversation in class. Now don't worry if you're a bit nervous about swimming. We'll take it very slowly, all right?'

'Yes, Miss,' Alice mumbled, going bright red.

She knew Miss Ritson was just trying to be nice. But it didn't help make the horrible feeling in her tummy any better.

Alice got into the pool, trying not to look at the others splashing around without a care. She remembered when it had been lots of fun too, before the girls at her old school started teasing her.

She moved along to stand with three

other girls who were nervously gripping the side and shivering.

Miss Ritson was blowing up orange armbands. She threw them to Alice's three classmates.

'I don't need armbands, Miss,' Alice said quickly.

Miss Ritson pointed to a pile of square white floats. 'You can use one of these, instead.'

'OK!' Alice quickly reached up and grabbed a float. Holding the float out in front with extended arms, she pushed gingerly off the side and kicked out with her legs.

'Very good, Alice. That's the way,' Miss Ritson called out encouragingly.

Alice swam slowly back and forth, doing widths with the float. She made sure not to go so quickly that Miss Ritson worked out that she was a good swimmer. None of the other girls paid Alice any attention, which was fine by her.

Letting herself drift, Alice glanced over towards the balcony cafe. Flame's tiny figure was curled up on one of the seats.

After quickly checking that no one was watching, Alice waved at him.

She saw Flame lift his head and prick
his ears, before jumping off the chair.
He leapt down the balcony steps and
came trotting purposefully down the
side of the pool.

*He must have thought I was waving to
him because I'm in trouble,* Alice thought.
I'd better go and tell him that I'm fine.

Bracing her hands on the edge of the
pool, she jumped up and heaved herself
out on to the side. As she was

straightening up, a group of boys came
out of the changing rooms and
surrounded Flame's invisible figure. Tim
Wagnall was one of them.

Alice tensed as she saw Flame trying
to navigate his way round the boys' legs.

Tim dug one of the others in the
ribs. 'Last one in the pool's a muppet!'
he cried.

'You're on!'

Tim and the other boy started
running.

One of the teachers blew her
whistle and gestured to them. 'Slow
down, you two!'

Tim waved to show he'd heard, but
as soon as the teacher turned back he
grinned mischievously and aimed a
play-kick at the boy beside him.

Flame had been just about to run past, when Tim's bare foot hit him and lifted him off his feet. He yowled with terror as he shot through the air and hurtled towards the pool!

Chapter
FIVE

Flame landed in the water with a tiny splash!

As he surfaced, Alice could see his tiny legs thrashing as he tried to stay afloat.

'Hey! Where did that kitten come from?' Tim cried.

Alice gasped. The shock must have made Flame forget to be invisible. Now he couldn't use his magic without giving himself away!

Without a second thought, Alice sprang off the side and dived in.

She kicked out strongly in a front crawl, cutting cleanly through the water. Her classmates lined the side of the pool, but she didn't notice.

She reached Flame's tiny soaked figure as he started to sink. Alice reached out, grabbed the scruff of his neck and yanked him to the surface. Flame whimpered in terror, coughing up water.

'I've got you now!' she said, drawing him close and treading water.

Flame seemed to be in a blind panic. He scrabbled at her arms, instinctively trying to find a safe foothold.

'Oh!' Alice gasped as his sharp claws raked her skin. She quickly flipped on to her back and settled him on her chest. 'Flame! Calm down,' she whispered.

Shivering and trembling, but calmer now, Flame lay on Alice's chest as she did a backstroke over to the steps.

As one of the teachers helped Alice climb out, a cheer went up. All the schoolkids were crowding round and clapping.

'She's saved that kitten!' someone cried.

'Did you see that brilliant dive?' said another kid.

'Way to go, Alice!' shouted Tim Wagnall.

Alice's cheeks burned. She wished they'd all stop making such a fuss. She was sure the teasing was about to start at any moment. Keeping her head down and holding Flame close, she pushed through them all.

'Not so fast, Alice! I want a word with you,' Miss Ritson stepped out to bar her way.

Alice nimbly wove round her and hurried towards the changing rooms. 'In a minute, Miss,' she shouted over her shoulder.

In the changing rooms, Alice threw herself into her cubicle and bolted the door. Grabbing her towel, she wrapped the shivering kitten in it and began gently patting him dry.

Flame began purring faintly. 'Thank you, Alice. You were very brave to dive in and rescue me. I know how you scared you have been.'

'I didn't really have time to think about it,' Alice realized. 'I just knew I couldn't bear it if anything happened to you.'

Now that all the excitement was over, her scratched arms began stinging. Alice winced at their soreness.

Flame's bright green eyes narrowed with concern. 'But I have hurt you. Let me make you better.'

Bright silver sparks appeared in
Flame's damp fur inside the towel, and
there was a faint crackling sound. The
tiny kitten leaned towards Alice and
huffed out a glittery mist. Alice felt

Flame's warm breath settle on her
scratches. The tingling increased for a
second and then suddenly all the pain
melted away and all sign of any
scratches faded.

'Come out of there at once, Alice!'
Miss Ritson ordered, sounding cross
and banging on the cubicle door. 'And
bring that kitten with you! Though
goodness only knows how it got into
here in the first place!'

'Uh-oh,' Alice whispered to Flame.
'Now I'm really for it. You'd better
make sure you stay invisible now.'

Flame nodded.

'Just coming, Miss,' Alice called,
buying herself some time.

Shivering, she draped her towel round
her head and shoulders. Alice took a

deep breath and unbolted the cubicle door.

Miss Ritson stood there with her hands on her hips. 'Are you ready to tell me what's going on now, Alice? And where's that kitten?'

'I don't know. It . . . um, ran off. It must be a stray or something,' Alice said, with her head bowed.

Miss Ritson peered into the cubicle suspiciously, but couldn't see Flame who was curled up invisibly on Alice's school jumper. 'I'll get someone to have a good look around for it, later. But what I'd really like to know, young lady, is how you changed from a nervous beginner into an excellent swimmer in about sixty seconds?'

Alice gulped, wracking her brains for something to say.

'I'm waiting,' Miss Ritson said.

'I . . . It must be a miracle,' Alice burst out. 'Yes, that's it! My thin blood has just got better all by itself. I bet it was the shock of diving in. As soon as I was in deep water, my arms and legs just started moving by themselves and suddenly – I could swim. Isn't it amazing? I'm definitely not sure it could ever happen again . . .' she gabbled.

'Alice,' Miss Ritson said warningly. 'I've had just about enough of this.'

Alice's shoulders slumped. She realized that it was time to tell her teacher the truth. 'I've . . . um, always been a good swimmer,' she admitted.

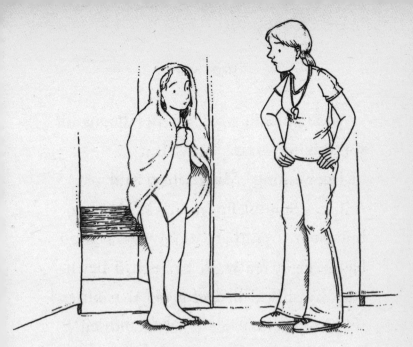

'Then why did you pretend you could hardly swim at all?'

'I didn't exactly say that. I just let you *think* I meant that,' Alice went on miserably. 'The thing is . . . I was the best swimmer in my class at my old school. And some of the girls thought I was showing off. They teased me about it all the time and so I started trying to get out of swimming lessons.'

Miss Ritson frowned. 'I understand

now. That must have been really awful for you,' she said gently. 'But not everyone gets jealous when they see others doing well. I'm certain that no one here is going to tease you. Your classmates were really impressed by the way you dived in and saved that kitten.'

'Were they?' Alice asked uncertainly, still having trouble making herself believe this.

'I can see that you're not convinced. I'll prove it to you,' Miss Ritson said. 'Come with me.'

Trying not to drag her feet, Alice nervously followed the teacher to the changing room door. Miss Ritson opened the door a crack, so that she and Alice could hear the other kids talking outside in the pool area.

'Did you see Alice's amazing dive?'

'Yeah! It was dead cool.'

'She's a fantastic swimmer. I hope she's in my team for the gala.'

Alice's eyes widened as she heard all the good comments. She finally realized that Miss Ritson was right. Her new classmates weren't jealous of her at all! She breathed a long-overdue sigh of relief as she realized that she was going

to be able to relax and enjoy her swimming lessons from now on.

Alice turned to the teacher. 'Thanks, Miss!' she said, her eyes shining.

'You're welcome. Just one more thing, before you get showered and changed,' Miss Ritson said seriously.

'Yes?'

'If you have any problems from now on, you'll speak to me or your mum about it. Promise?'

Alice blushed, but she felt a grin stretching from ear to ear. 'Promise!' she agreed.

Chapter
★ SIX ★

'Everyone's talking about how you dived into the pool to save a grey and white kitten. It was Flame, wasn't it?' Ben said, as he and Alice walked home after the bell had gone.

'Er . . . yeah. He must have jumped into my school bag when I wasn't looking,' Alice said hastily. 'But . . . I . . . er, ran home at lunchtime and took him back up to my bedroom.'

Ben dragged his school bag on the floor behind him. 'I never get to spend time with Flame,' he complained.

Alice realized this was true. All she seemed to do lately, where Flame was concerned, was tell Ben off. 'How

would you like him to sleep on your bed tonight?' *I'm sure Flame won't mind*, she thought.

'Cool! And can I feed him too?' Ben asked, beaming all over his face.

Alice smiled. 'Course you can!'

Over the next few days Ben was really careful to be gentle with Flame. He helped Alice smuggle food up to her bedroom for him and was delighted when Flame slept on his bed for a second night.

'I've washed Flame's food bowl,' Ben said to Alice, one evening just before bedtime. 'We have to be careful Mum doesn't see it.'

Alice smiled. Ben hadn't sulked for ages and was being really protective of

Flame now. 'Thanks, Ben. See you in the morning,' she said.

'Night, Alice.'

The following morning, Flame lay stretched out on Alice's duvet, looking relaxed and content as she was getting ready for school.

'I'm getting on well with everyone in swimming lessons now,' Alice said. 'I don't have to worry being teased at all and I can just concentrate on improving my stroke.'

Flame nodded. 'You are a very good swimmer, Alice.'

'Thanks! I'm not bad,' she said modestly.

The extra practice at the after–school club was helping too. Her mum was happy for her to go along for an hour on two evenings a week.

Today was Monday and Alice felt excited and a tiny bit nervous. Miss Ritson was going to be picking the teams for the swimming gala first thing before normal lessons started.

She finished putting on her school shoes. 'Come on, Flame. Let's go and get some breakfast! I want to get to school early to make sure I get picked for lots of teams.'

Flame gave an extra loud purr and trotted after Alice. Out on the landing she bumped into her mum going into the bathroom. Mrs Forester was still in her dressing gown. She looked pale and tired.

'Are you OK, Mum?' Alice asked worriedly.

Her mum shook her head carefully.
'I've woken up with a splitting
headache. I'm going to have to take
a painkiller.'

'Poor you,' Alice sympathized. 'Why
don't you go back to bed and I'll bring
you up a cup of tea? Don't worry

about us. I'll get Ben's breakfast and get him ready for school.'

'Thanks, love, you're a star,' her mum said, smiling weakly. 'Just give me half an hour. I'll be fine by the time Esme and Luke arrive. Oh, I've just remembered. Ben's school shirt needs ironing.'

'No problem!' Alice said, going downstairs into the kitchen.

After taking the tea up to her mum, she got out the ironing board. As Alice was sorting a shirt out of the pile of ironing, Ben came into the kitchen.

'Where's Mum?' he asked.

Alice explained about the headache.

'Oh. Can I have toast with egg on for breakfast?' Ben asked.

'Sorry. I haven't got time to make that. Can you have cereal?'

'If I have to.' Ben went to the cupboard and took out a packet of Chocco Blasts. He rattled the packet. 'This is nearly empty. And I don't like anything else.' He stamped over to the table and sat there with his chin in his hands. 'I s'pose I'll just have to starve,' he moaned.

Alice sighed. She didn't need this right now.

She felt a tiny paw pat her ankle and looked down to see Flame beckoning to her to follow him. The moment he scampered into the utility room, there was a tiny flash and a fountain of sparks.

A plastic shopping bag appeared out

of thin air. Inside it was a mega-sized packet of Chocco Blasts.

'Wow! Thanks, Flame. But could you make the packet a bit small–' she began and then she stopped hurriedly as Ben came in.

He immediately spotted the enormous box of cereal. 'Hey! Brilliant!

Mum must have got these on special offer!' Wrapping both arms round the box, he went into the kitchen with it.

'Let me help you pour some out,' Alice said, following him.

'I want to do it!' Ben exclaimed.

He tore open the box and aimed it awkwardly at the empty bowl. A landslide of Chocco Blasts shot out.

They overflowed the bowl, piled up on the kitchen table and shot all over the floor with a spattering noise.

'Oh, great! Now I'll have to hoover that lot up as well!' Alice grumbled.

Ben wasn't listening. 'This is ace!' he said, sloshing milk about and shovelling chocolate cereal into his mouth.

'I am sorry, Alice. I was trying to help,' Flame mewed softly.

'I know you were. Never mind. At least Ben's happy!' she whispered, going back to ironing his shirt.

Ten minutes and three bowls of cereal later, Ben got down from the table. He had a sticky rim of chocolate-coloured drool round his mouth. 'Don't feel very well,' he murmured.

'I'm not surprised. You've been scoffing for England!' Alice said, wiping his mouth with kitchen roll. 'Put this shirt on and don't you dare be sick!'

As Ben finished dressing and then went off to fetch his school things, Alice heard her mum moving about upstairs. 'Oh heck! Mum's getting up. She must be feeling better. I'll never have time to clear this up!'

'Do not worry,' Flame purred. He pointed a tiny front paw and there was another crackle as a fountain of sparks shot towards the table. The packet of Chocco Blasts shrank to normal size and with a fizzing sound all the spilled cereal and pools of milk melted away.

'Phew! Thanks, Flame. Quick, can you jump into my school bag? Let's grab Ben and get off to school before he says anything to Mum!'

Chapter
★ SEVEN ★

'. . . and finally, Tim Wagnall and Alice
Forester. That makes up the relay team,'
Miss Ritson said, finishing choosing
teams for all the races.

'Yay!' Alice cried, jumping up and
down. She was also in the girls'
breaststroke, the mixed front crawl and
the inter-class race, but her all-time
favourite was the relay race.

She glanced over to where Flame was curled up on the window sill. Quickly checking that no one was looking, she gave him a sneaky thumbs-up.

'The grand pool opening is next Saturday, so it'll be closed on Friday to get ready for the celebrations. We've a special guest coming to do the honours. Judy Blasket.'

'She's an actress from *Ivygreen* – my mum's favourite TV soap! Just wait until I tell her,' Alice said excitedly.

'We're hoping Judy will attract a big crowd!' Miss Ritson smiled. 'Right everyone, you have four days to practise your swimming, including today's lesson. So collect your kit and we'll go straight across to the pool.'

'Great! Come on, team. Let's grab a relay baton and start practising!' Tim jumped up and did one of his front crawl impressions across the room and out into the corridor.

The other kids laughed, but Alice couldn't bring herself to join in. She still hadn't quite forgiven Tim for kicking Flame into the pool. She knew it was an accident, but it wouldn't have happened if Tim wasn't always acting the fool.

'Can you stay in the balcony cafe this time? I don't want anything else to happen to you,' she whispered to Flame.

Flame nodded and gave her a furry grin. 'I do not feel like going in the pool again!'

As Miss Ritson blew her whistle for the end of the lesson, Alice climbed out of the pool.

Her muscles ached, but she didn't feel a bit tired. She'd swum really well today. In relay practice, she'd passed the baton smoothly at each change-over. She couldn't wait for the gala on Saturday.

'Well done, Alice. I'm glad to see you enjoying yourself,' Miss Ritson commented. 'I think I picked the right girl for our relay team.'

Alice beamed at her. 'Hope so, Miss!'

Some of the kids were grabbing their towels from the radiators, where they'd left them earlier, and going up to get hot drinks from the machine in the cafe.

Alice wrapped herself in her warm towel and also headed for the balcony.

She was looking forward to telling Flame how great swimming had been today.

But when she reached the cafe, she couldn't see him anywhere. She checked beneath all the chairs and tables, but there was no sign of him.

Maybe he was waiting for her in the changing rooms. Alice went straight back to her cubicle. But Flame wasn't there either.

After showering and dressing in double-quick time, Alice hurried back to the classroom and arrived before everybody else. She looked for Flame on the window sill and the tops of the cupboards.

But there was still no sign of him.

After checking under all the desks, Alice sank into her seat. She wasn't sure what to do next. 'Flame? Where are you?' she said out loud, worried.

There was a very faint whimper. It sounded as if it came from inside her shoulder bag.

'Flame?' Picking up her bag, Alice slipped her hand inside. 'Ah, there you are . . .' Her fingers brushed against a tightly curled furry little bundle.

She was so glad to have found him that she took a moment to realize that the tiny kitten was trembling all over. Alice felt a stir of alarm as she opened the bag up wider. A pair of troubled emerald eyes glowed at her from the interior.

'What's wrong? Are you sick?' she asked gently.

'My uncle's spies are very close,'
Flame whined in terror.

Alice bit back a gasp. The moment
she had been dreading was here. Flame
was in terrible danger. Even though she
hated to think of losing her friend, she
knew she was going to have to be
strong.

'Are . . . are you leaving now?' she
asked.

Flame shook his head. 'I will hide in

here. My enemies may pass me by and then I will be able to stay.'

'Right! We're leaving! I'll find somewhere else to hide you. I just have to think of something to tell Miss Ritson.' Alice decided.

'No, Alice. That would just draw attention to me,' he interrupted. 'Just leave me here for a little while.' Flattening his ears, Flame curled into an even tighter ball.

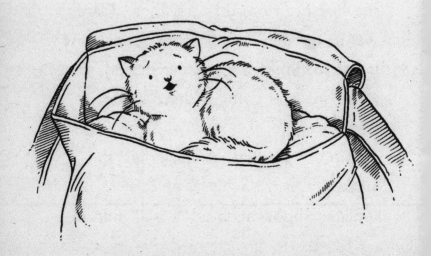

'All right,' Alice whispered.

As her classmates began filing into the room, Alice tucked the bag with the terrified kitten inside under her desk.

Alice's chest felt tight as she tried to push away the horrid thought that Flame could still be found at any moment. She didn't know how she was going to concentrate on her work, but there was nothing else she could do.

Chapter
★EIGHT★

Alice hardly dared look inside her school bag. Somehow she resisted checking on Flame until it was time to go home.

Her heart was beating fast as she opened her bag.

Flame had gone.

'Oh!' Alice gasped, biting back tears. She felt a wave of sadness wash over her. She hadn't even said a proper goodbye.

Alice went to meet Ben. As they walked home together, she felt as if she was in a daze.

'Are you OK?' Ben asked worriedly.

Alice nodded. 'I'm just tired, that's all.' She didn't feel up to telling him about Flame yet.

Back home, she dumped her coat and bag in the hall and went straight upstairs. Ben was just coming out of her bedroom.

'What are you doing in my room?' she snapped, before she could stop herself.

Ben blinked at her in surprise. 'I was only saying hello to Flame. I'm going downstairs to watch TV now.'

'I'm sorry, Ben. I didn't mean to shout at –' Alice stopped and did a double take. 'Did you say – Flame?'

'Yeah,' Ben said, giving her a funny look.

Alice shot into her room. Flame was sitting on her duvet washing his grey and white fur. He looked up as she came in and she saw that the tip of his tiny pink tongue was still hanging out.

'Oh, Flame. You came back!' she exclaimed, giving him a cuddle.

An enormous happy grin spread over Alice's face. She thought she might burst with happiness.

'I laid a false trail and escaped my uncle's spies,' Flame purred. 'But if they come again, I may have to leave at once.'

'I'm just glad you're here now!' Alice said.

Flame's bright emerald eyes crinkled in a smile. 'So am I. I am looking forward to watching you swim in the school gala!'

Alice felt excited as she and Flame, her mum and Ben walked through the school gates on Saturday and joined the crowds already there.

Strings of coloured bunting and bunches of balloons hung outside the pool building. A huge banner read 'Meldway School Swimming Pool, Grand Opening.'

Alice saw a smart car draw up. A pretty blonde woman, wearing bright make-up, a jade green dress and lots of jewellery, got out.

'That's the actress from Mum's soap,' she whispered to Flame.

Flame was in her school bag. He had his head sticking out and was watching everything with great interest.

Everyone cheered as Judy Blasket smiled and waved. The headmaster gave a speech and then the glamorous actress cut the ribbon and declared the new pool open.

As a man from the local paper began taking photos, Alice and Flame and all the other children taking part in the gala went inside to get changed.

'See you in there!' Alice called to her mum and Ben.

'All right, love!' Mrs Forester called from the queue of people waiting to get Judy Blasket's autograph.

In the changing rooms, excited voices filled the air. The whole of Alice's year was taking part in the gala, so she had to share a cubicle with a classmate.

'Where are you going to be today?' she whispered to Flame worriedly, once the other girl had gone out.

'I found a safe ledge to sit on when I was laying a false trail for my enemies,' Flame mewed.

'OK. I'll see you after the gala. Wish me luck!' Alice picked Flame up. Breathing in his sweet kitten smell, she kissed the top of his head.

'Good luck, Alice,' Flame said with an extra big purr.

As Alice emerged from the foot bath, she saw that the pool looked even bigger and more impressive with seats lining the sides and so many people watching. The balcony cafe was full of spectators too.

Alice's tummy did a flip with nerves and excitement. But it was a good feeling. She never would have dreamed that she'd be swimming in front of all these people *and* have her new classmates cheering her on.

The races began and the sound of cheers and splashing echoed around the building. Then it was time for Alice's first race, the girls' breaststroke.

She had butterflies in her tummy as she lined up with the other competitors.

'Take your marks! Ready!'

Ph-eeep! As the whistle blew Alice flung herself into a dive. She surfaced and started swimming. Her nerves faded instantly and all she could think about was swimming to the finish as fast as possible.

A cheer went up as the race ended. Alice had come third. She was third in the mixed front crawl and joint second with the rest of her class in the inter-class race.

In between watching the other races, Alice glanced to the back of the pool where she could see Flame's tiny figure sitting below one of the tall windows.

Flame saw her looking. He waved a tiny front paw and a cloud of bright pink sparks shot out. They floated

upwards and briefly formed the shape
of a glittering pink butterfly.

Alice smiled as the butterfly fluttered
over towards her. She held up her hand
and the butterfly settled for a moment,
before dissolving into glittering, invisible
dust.

'Thanks, Flame,' Alice breathed. It was
good to know that he was supporting
her in his own special way.

The relay race was the final race of
the day.

Alice stood ready with her other
team members. One of the boys went
first, followed by a girl. Alice watched
tensely. Her team was starting to fall
behind. There were about three metres
to make up already.

Then it was Tim's turn. As their team

member swam to the side, Tim Wagnall got ready to take the baton. He leaned out and went to grasp it.

'Oh,' Alice gasped. Tim had dropped the baton!

'Quick, jump in and get it!' she urged.

Tim jumped in. He splashed about and finally grabbed the floating baton. Pushing off the side he started swimming.

Alice's spirits sank as Tim swam to the deep end and then turned to swim back. He tried his best, but by the time he raised the baton for Alice to take it, he was half a length behind everyone else.

Alice was never going to be able to make up the distance.

Alice leaned out and grasped the baton. Yes! She had it. Holding it tight, she hurled herself into a shallow dive. As she surfaced, she was already stretching out in a powerful front crawl.

Kicking her legs and concentrating on her over-arm stroke, she powered towards the deep end. Gritting her teeth, Alice swam as if her life depended on it. At the turn, she was barely two metres behind the leader.

As she swam back towards the finish, Alice gradually drew level with the lead swimmer.

'Come on, Alice!' yelled Tim.

'You can do it!' shouted Miss Ritson.

Three metres to the finish! Alice and the lead swimmer were neck and neck. Alice used every last bit of her strength in a final spurt. She stretched out and her fingers touched the edge a micro-second before the other girl.

She'd won the race for her team!

'Yes!' Alice threw her arms in the air.

Cheers and clapping broke out as Alice climbed out of the pool. She couldn't stop smiling.

'Well done!' Mrs Forester shouted. Alice looked over to see her mum and Ben hugging each other and jumping up and down. She waved at them.

Alice's team members congratulated her. Tim Wagnall looked about to throw his arms round her neck.

'Woah!' Alice took a step back. That was going *too* far!

Tim got the message. 'That was *so* brilliant. You're a great swimmer – for a soppy girl!' he joked.

Alice shook her head. Tim would never change. But she would still rather be in this class in her new school than anywhere else!

Alice was glad that Flame was safe up on his window ledge. There was no way that she could sneak over to see him with all the fuss still going on.

After the applause died down, there
was a break before the prize-giving.
Alice slipped away to wash her hair.
Most people had stayed where they were
and the changing rooms were empty.

As Alice took off her cap and went to
fetch her shampoo from her cubicle,
there was a blinding white flash.

'Oh!' she gasped, rubbing her eyes.

Flame stood there, looking
magnificent as his true lion self.
Silver sparkles glittered in his thick
white fur. This time, next to Flame,
there stood an older grey lion with a
wise expression.

And then Alice knew that her friend
was really leaving this time. 'Your
enemies have come back, haven't they?'
she asked, her voice breaking.

'Yes, they have. And now I must go,'
Flame's deep gentle voice rumbled.

Alice ran forward and threw her
arms round Flame's muscular neck.
'I'm really going to miss you. I'll never
forget you!' she said tearfully. She forced
herself to stand back. 'Go! Quickly!
Save yourself!'

Flame nodded. 'You have been a good
friend. Be well, Alice.'

The old grey lion smiled at Alice and there was a last bright flash and a burst of sparks that showered down round her and sizzled on the wet tiles. Flame and the grey lion faded and then finally disappeared.

Alice stood there, her heart aching and her throat tight with tears.

'Alice! There you are!' called one of her classmates. 'Miss Ritson sent me to find you. The prize-giving's about to start.'

'I'll be one minute!' Alice took a deep breath as she thought about the adventure she had shared with the magic kitten. Flame would be her special secret forever.

As Alice went back towards the swimming pool, she looked at her team and the prize they were about to receive and a proud smile pushed away her sadness.

Magic Kitten

Picture Perfect

Flame needs to find a purrfect new friend!

And that's how Orla
believes her dream of
winning the photo
competition could
come true when little
chocolate-brown kitten
Flame comes into the
picture . . .

puffin.co.uk

A Puzzle of Paws
Flame needs to find a purrfect new friend!

And that's how Rosie's worries about moving house get easier to bear when cuddly black kitten Flame becomes part of the furniture . . .

A Shimmering Splash

Flame needs to find a purrfect new friend!

And that's how the sun
suddenly shines on Lorna's
gloomy island stay when
playful amber and white
kitten Flame comes ashore . . .

Coming Soon . . .

A Christmas Surprise
978–0–141–32323–7

puffin.co.uk

A Summer Spell
9780141320144

Classroom Chaos
9780141320151

Star Dreams
9780141320168

Double Trouble
9780141320175

Moonlight Mischief
9780141321530

A Circus Wish
9780141321547

Sparkling Steps
9780141321554

A Glittering Gal
9780141321561

Seaside Mystery
9780141321981

Firelight Friends
9780141321998

A Shimmering Splash
9780141322001

A Puzzle of Paw
9780141322018

A Christmas Surprise
9780141323237

Picture Perfect
9780141323480

A Splash of Fo
97801413234

Win a Magic Kitten goody bag!

An urgent and secret message has been left for Flame
from his own world, where his evil uncle is
still hunting for him.

Four words from the message can be found in
royal lion crowns hidden in *A Splash of Forever*
Find the hidden words and put them together to complete
the message. Send it in to us and each month we will
put every correct message in a draw and pick out one lucky
winner who will receive a purrfect Magic Kitten gift!

Send your secret message, name and address on a postcard to:
Magic Kitten Competition
Puffin Books
80 Strand
London WC2R 0RL

Hurry, Flame needs your help!

Good luck!

Magic Puppy

Magic Puppy
A New Beginning
SUE BENTLEY

A New Beginning
9780141323503

Magic Puppy
Muddy Paws
SUE BENTLEY

Muddy Paws
9780141323510

Magic Puppy
Cloud Capers
SUE BENTLEY

Cloud Capers
9780141323527

Magic Puppy
Star of the show
SUE BENTLEY

Star of the Show
9780141323534

puffin.co.uk